MW01167155

REVERSE RAPTURE BOOKS

GLAD TIDINGS FOR THE RIGHT AND THE LEFT BEHIND

CLEVELAND • SAN FRANCISCO

www.reverserapture.com

To Monkey, for making it all possible!

Alison Bechdel is a genius.

FIRST EDITION: NOVEMBER 2007

10 9 8 7 6 5 4 3 2 1

LIBRARY OF CONGRESS CATALOGING-IN-PUBLICATION DATA

PHILIPS, IAN.
THE RAPTURE FOR BIG SINNERS: 66 + 6 THINGS TO DO BEFORE & AFTER THE RIGHTEOUS LIFT OFF / SCRIBBLED & DOODLED BY IAN PHILIPS.

p. cm.

ISBN-13: 978-0-9789023-2-2 (hard cover)
ISBN-10: 0-9789023-2-7 (hard cover)

1. Religion-- Humor. 2. Rapture (Christian eschatology)-- Humor.
I. Title.

PN6231.R4P45 2007
818'.607 -- dc 22   2007019516

REVERSE RAPTURE BOOKS. AN IMPRINT OF SUSPECT THOUGHTS PRESS • 2215-R MARKET ST, PMB 544, SAN FRANCISCO, CA 94114-1612 • www.myspace.com/reverserapture

the RAPTURE

FOR Big Sinners

66 + 6 THINGS TO DO BEFORE & AFTER
THE RIGHTEOUS LIFT OFF

scribbled & doodled by ian philips
with felix rumpus

LEAVE ME BEHIND—
PLEASE!

REVERSE RAPTURE BOOKS

CLEVELAND · SAN FRANCISCO

CHAPTER 1

YOU MUST BE THIS BAD ~~/~~

TO READ

THIS BOOK :

⸺

OKAY, THAT'S SETTING
THE BAR TOO HIGH.

THIS BAD :

SEVERE

SEVERE RISK OF DAMNATION

HITLER, STALIN & ANY OTHER ASSHOLE COMMITTING GENOCIDE

HIGH

HIGH RISK OF DAMNATION

CONCEIVED OF MANAGED HEALTH CARE AND/OR SUBPRIME LENDING AND/OR OUTSOURCING AND/OR ARE ROGER AILES

ELEVATED

SIGNIFICANT RISK OF DAMNATION

PARTICIPATED IN PRODUCTION OF THE MOVIE VERSION OF THE DA VINCI CODE

GUARDED

~~GENERAL~~ **RISK OF DAMNATION**

DE-GAYED THE REV. TED HAGGARD IN JUST 21 DAYS (HASTE MAKES WASTE!)

LOW

LOW RISK OF DAMNATION

CONVINCED BRITNEY SPEARS TO SHAVE HER HEAD & GO COMMANDO WITH PARIS HILTON

HELLO, BAD BOYS AND GIRLS!
OH, STOP RIGHT NOW. NO MORE BLEATS
OF MOCK OUTRAGE. NO MORE CROCODILE
TEARS. BOTH YOU AND I KNOW THAT
GOOD BOYS AND GIRLS WOULD NEVER
READ A BOOK LIKE THIS — AND THAT'S
WHY THEY ARE SO FRIGHTFULLY
BORING!

MY NAME IS MR. RUMPUS. AND
I'LL BE YOUR TOUR GUIDE THROUGH
RAPTUREVILLE.

tRIBULATION tours

No, I'm not a knockoff faun. I'm a satyr. Distant cousins. Very distant as my kind don't throw our hooves in the air for you know who. No, not Lord Voldemort, sillies. And not Aslan. Jesus. We satyrs play the field when it comes to deities. Whoever keeps our hooves shiny and our horns hard, we love,

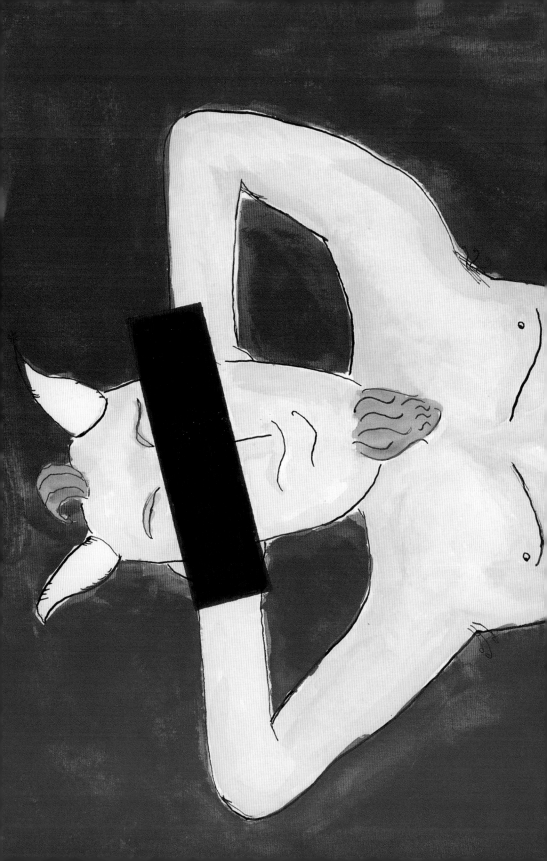

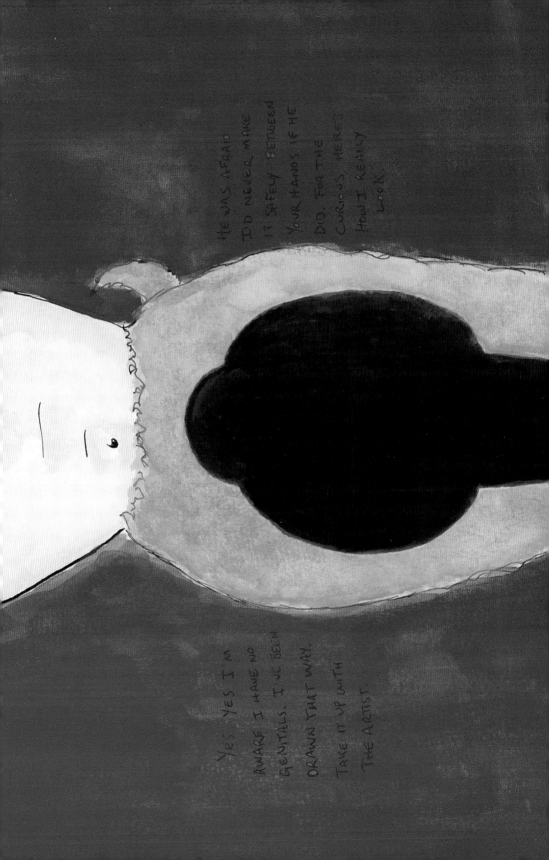

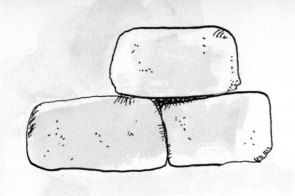

BESIDES YOURS TRULY, OUR CAST OF CHARACTERS INCLUDES THE NAMELESS (AND MOSTLY FACE-LESS) DAMNED. (THAT'S YOU, DEARIE.) DON'T BELIEVE ME? JUST HAVE A LOOK IN THE MIRROR.

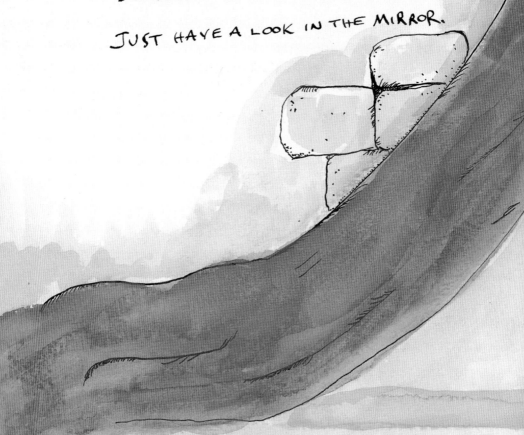

AND THIS GAGGLE OF WHITE
BORN-AGAIN PROTESTANTS, THE
PARSONS CLAN:

ALAN   LOUELLA   LUCY

GRAHAM

OUR LAZY ARTIST CAN'T BE BOTHERED
TO DRAW ALL THE RIGTHEOUS, SO HE
FIGURES THIS FAMILY CAN STAND IN FOR
THE LOT OF THEM.

NOW THAT WE KNOW THE PLAYERS,
IT'S ON WITH THE SHOW!

CHAPTER 2

A CHILD'S OVERVIEW
OF THE
RAPTURE

or

RAPTURE 101

OH, MY. I'M FORGETTING MY AUDIENCE. BIG SINNERS ARE A VERY HIP CROWD. NOTHING BUT SPLIT SCREENS AND LOUD EXPLOSIONS AND IRONY WILL DO.

HEAVEN-BOUND BABYCAM

PURGATORY-BOUND DIAPERCAM

HELL-BOUND MOTHERCAM

WELL, SO MUCH FOR THE CHILD'S OVERVIEW.
NOW, LET'S GET ON WITH AN OVERVIEW
SIMPLE ENOUGH FOR A CHILD. EVEN A
WICKED CHILD, LIKE YOURSELF.

THE BEST WAY TO TELL YOU WHAT
THE RAPTURE IS
IS TO TELL YOU WHAT IT ISN'T.

• IT'S NOT THE FILM THAT'S MOST
MEMORABLE FOR STARRING THE
POKER-ACE EX OF TOM CRUISE
AND DAVID DUCHOVNY'S ASS.

HIS MULLET, TOO

• IT'S NOT THE BOOK-LENGTH
LESBIAN LOVE POEM BY CAROL
ANN DUFFY.

• IT'S NOT THE DISCO-PUNK BAND
FROM BROOKLYN.

• AND IT'S CERTAINLY NOT A CERTAIN
SONG SPILLING THE BEANS ON A
CENTURIES-OLD CONSPIRACY TO KEEP
SECRET THE WILD GOINGS-ON IN THE
PRIVATE LIFE OF JESUS.

SO, WHAT IS THE RAPTURE THEN? IN A NUT-
SHELL, IT'S THE OPENING CREDITS OF THE
APOCALYPSE.

APOCALYPSE? NOW? TELL US MORE,
YOU CRY.

THAT'S ANOTHER BOOK, MY DEARIES.
(HINT, HINT: GIVE THIS BOOK TO ALL THE
MISFIT TOYS AND WEIRDOS YOU ~~KNOW~~
THINK ARE REALLY BIG SINNERS. THIS
ARTIST REFUSES TO DRAW ME UNLESS
HE'S WELL-FED.)

BUT I'LL GIVE YOU A ~~WITHHOLD~~ CLUE. APOCALYPSE
IS GREEK FOR THE BOOK OF REVELATION.
OKAY, NOT REALLY. BUT ISN'T THAT
SUCCINCT.

BOOK OF REVELATION? REALLY NOW, KIDDIES,
IF YOU'RE GOING TO BE DAMNED YOU MIGHT
AS WELL KNOW WHY.

CLASS, TURN TO THE LAST CHAPTER OF OUR
                                BIBLES.

HARPY —
NOT TO BE
CONFUSED
WITH
HAPPY —
THE BABY
NEW YEAR —
IN RUDOLPH'S
SHINY NEW
YEAR

ACTUALLY, THEY'RE PUTTI — KIND OF LIKE ANGEL
FETUSES. BUT DON'T TELL THEM THAT. THEY
THINK THEY'RE HARD-CORE — AND FULL GROWN.

AND A LOT OF AMERICANS BELIEVE IN THE
DOOM AND GLOOM OF THE BOOK OF REVELATION.
SURVEY SAYS 59%. (SOURCE: AN HONEST-TO-
GOD TIME/CNN POLL FROM 2002.)

WHO CARES WHAT AMERICANS THINK?
MOSTLY AMERICANS... AND THE REST OF THE
WORLD — BUT ONLY BECAUSE THEY KNOW
AMERICA HAS THE MOST BELIEVERS WHO'RE
REVVED FOR THE PLANET TO BLOW AND THE MOST
BOMBS TO DO THE JOB.

OF COURSE, EARTH EXPLODING LIKE THE
DEATH STAR (I AND II) ISN'T REALLY WHAT
THE APOCALYPSE IS ABOOT. IT'S ABOUT A
WORLD CONSUMED BY FLAMES, BLOOD, AND
DEATH. THE ORIGINAL GLOBAL WARMING.
BUT THE PLANET STAYS INTACT. FOR THE
APOCALYPSE NEEDS A STAGE FOR THE BATTLE
OF ARMAGEDDON AND THE RETURN OF
THE KING.

NO, NOT ELVIS. I WISH. JESUS, SILLIES.

CHAPTER 2.5

THE BEASTIE BOYS —
THE SLOUCHING FROM BABYLON TO BAGHDAD TOUR

SO WHAT'S IN THE BOOK OF REVELATION?
HONIES, WHAT ISN'T! IT'S GOT FOUR HORSEMEN
AND SEVEN KILLER SEALS AND BLOOD- SPOUTING
LAMBS AND HORNY DRAGONS AND BLOOD AND FIRE
AND ANGEL ARMIES AND GOG AND MAGOG AND
THE WHORE OF BABLYON (AND NO, IT'S NOT
MADONNA OR HILLARY RODHAM CLINTON —
NOT EVEN ANN COULTER, SHE WISHES.)

BASICALLY, IT'S A PLAY-BY- PLAY OF THE ALL- WORLD
GENOCIDE, OTHERWISE KNOWN AS THE TRIBULATION,
NEEDED BEFORE JESUS WILL DO A WALK-ON AND
STAY PUT FOR A THOUSAND YEARS. (AND YOU
THOUGHT MADONNA WAS A DIVA!)

HERE'S A HANDY ROGUES GALLERY OF
WHO'S WHO IN THE BOOK OF REVELATION:

REV 1 : 10 - 17   THE ALPHA ANGEL

CECI N'EST
PAS LE PETIT
PRINCE.

REV 4 : 6 - 8
GOD'S LAPDOGS

GLORY,
GLORY,
GLORY

THANK YOU,
JESUS!

REV 6 : 1 - 8

THE FOUR HORSEMEN OF
OMICRON THETA
(SEE CHAPTER 2.5½)

REV 5 : 1   THE 7 SEALS

HAPPY   GRUMPY   DOPEY   SNEEZY   BASH-FUL   DOC   SLEEPY

REV 10 : 8-11
SWEET & SOUR BOOK

REV 11 : 3-12
THE TWO WITNESSES

REV 12 : 1
THE WOMAN WITH THE MOON & STARS

REV 16 : 1-21
7 VIALS FOR 7 ANGELS

REV 17 : 1 - 18
THE WHORE OF BABYLON

YOU THINK THIS SHOWS BABS IN HER TRUE COLORS — HA — WRITE NIGHTSWEATS & T-CELLS (www.nightsweats.com) AND BEG GIL TO MAKE YOU A "FAMILY FIRST" SHIRT.

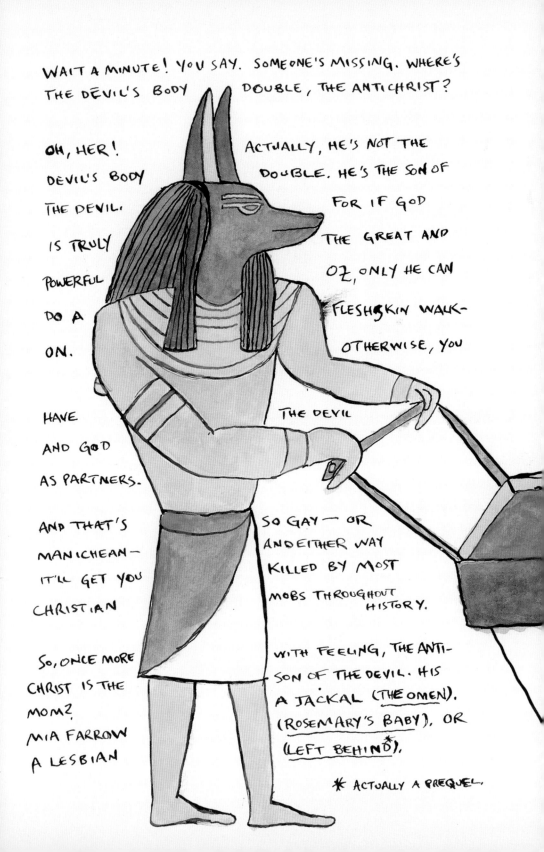

WAIT A MINUTE! YOU SAY. SOMEONE'S MISSING. WHERE'S THE DEVIL'S BODY DOUBLE, THE ANTICHRIST?

OH, HER! DEVIL'S BODY THE DEVIL. IS TRULY POWERFUL DO A ON.

ACTUALLY, HE'S NOT THE DOUBLE. HE'S THE SON OF FOR IF GOD THE GREAT AND OZ, ONLY HE CAN FLESH&SKIN WALK- OTHERWISE, YOU

THE DEVIL

HAVE AND GOD AS PARTNERS.

AND THAT'S MANICHEAN— IT'LL GET YOU CHRISTIAN

SO, ONCE MORE CHRIST IS THE MOM? MIA FARROW A LESBIAN

SO GAY — OR AND EITHER WAY KILLED BY MOST MOBS THROUGHOUT HISTORY.

WITH FEELING, THE ANTI- SON OF THE DEVIL. HIS A JACKAL (THE OMEN). (ROSEMARY'S BABY), OR (LEFT BEHIND).

* ACTUALLY A PREQUEL.

STILL, IT'S A GOOD QUESTION. WHERE IS THE ANTICHRIST? ACCORDING TO MANY EVANGELICAL CHRISTIANS, HE HIDING IN PLAIN SIGHT RIGHT NOW.

BUT HOW WILL WE RECOGNIZE HIM? YOU WAIL. WE WANT TO JOIN UP.

WELL, MOST LIKELY HE'LL FIND YOU. YOU SEE, HE'S HARD TO PIN DOWN.

OVER THE LAST 2,000 YEARS HE'S BEEN A JEW (THE DEVIL'S GOD'S BIGGEST COPYCAT, DON'T YOU KNOW), A GIANT (LEAVE IT TO THE IRISH), EVEN A ZOMBIE EMPEROR NERO (I SHIT YOU NOT).

BUT YOU WILL KNOW HIM BY HIS WORKS. HE CAN DO MIRACLES. LIKE BEING UNIVERSALLY ADORED. AND UNITING EARTH UNDER ONE WORLD GOVERNMENT. (HE ONLY TURNS NASTY ONCE THAT'S IN PLACE AND DECLARES HIMSELF GOD ON TEMPLE MOUNT IN JERUSALEM AND STAMPS EVERYBODY WITH THE MARK OF THE BEAST— IF YOU DON'T GET ONE, YOU CAN'T BUY OR SELL ANYTHING — EVEN ON EBAY. AND WE CAN'T HAVE THAT, CAN WE?! AND, IN TIME, HE'LL HAVE YOUR HEAD CHOPPED OFF. CHRISTIANS FIRST, OF COURSE.)

THAT'S ALL WELL AND GOOD, YOU SAY. BUT THAT PART ABOUT BEING UNI- VERSALLY ADORED? YOU ASK. WHO COULD PULL THAT OFF? WHO SHOULD I BE ON THE LOOKOUT FOR?

WE FED KEY PASSAGES FROM THE BOOK OF REVELATION INTO A HIGH-POWERED CRIME- FIGHTING COMPUTER FROM THE DEPARTMENT OF HOMELAND SECURITY. WE ALSO ADDED IMAGES OF HIGHLY BELOVED ICONS FROM AROUND THE WORLD. BASED ON THE BEST TECHNOLOGY THE WORLD POSSESSES, WE CAME UP WITH THIS ARTIST'S SKETCH!

CHAPTER 2.5 ½

RAPTURE ME THIS

THAT'S ALL WELL AND GOOD, YOU SAY. BUT THEY'RE ALL POST-RAPTURE, RIGHT?

YES, INDEED. THE TRIBULATION HAS NOTHING TO DO WITH CUTE FUZZY-WUZZY TRIBBLES.

SO THEN, YOU CRY, WHAT DOES THE BOOK OF REVELATION HAVE TO SAY ABOUT THE RAPTURE?

NADA.

YOU MEAN IT'S A SECRET? YOU ASK.

NO SECRET. NO MYSTERY.

IT'S JUST NOT THERE.

DANCING ANGELS- THE ORIGINAL ~~TREKKIES~~ TREKKERS

(NOW, NOT TO GET ANGELS DANCING ON THE HEADS OF PINS, BUT 1 THESSALONIANS 4:17 DOES MENTION A MIDAIR MEETING OF THE LIVING WITH CHRIST RIGHT AFTER THE DEAD HAVE RISEN IN THE DIVINE EQUIVALENT OF A SENIOR CITIZEN DISCOUNT. THE GREEK WORD FOR THIS LIFT OFF IS HARPAZO, WHICH GOT TRANSLATED INTO LATIN AS THE WORD THAT'S THE ROOT FOR OUR WORD "RAPTURE." BUT MANY ESCHATOLOGISTS - THAT'S FANCY-PANTS TALK FOR NERDS OBSESSED WITH EARTH DOING A SOLO "BIG BANG"- PUT THE DEAD RISING AFTER THE TRIBULATION WHILE THE RAPTURE WE'RE LEARNING ABOUT GOES BY THE CHATROOM HANDLE OF "PRE-TRIBULATION RAPTURE.")

BUT JUST BECAUSE IT'S NOT THERE NEVER STOPPED A LOT OF PEOPLE FROM BELIEVING IN IT.

SOME SAY THE NOTION OF THE RAPTURE COMES FROM ST. PAUL, THAT ONE-STOP SOURCE OF ALL THINGS WARM AND FUZZY IN CHRISTIANITY, AND YES, THE "OFFICIAL" AUTHOR OF 1 THESSALONIANS 4:17. IF NOT THAT PASSAGE, RAPTURE-ENTHUSIASTS LIKE TO CITE THIS CHAPTER AND VERSE, 1 CORINTHIANS 15:52:

"IN A MOMENT, IN THE TWINKLING OF AN EYE, AT THE LAST TRUMP: FOR THE TRUMPET SHALL SOUND, AND THE DEAD SHALL BE RAISED, INCORRUPTIBLE, AND WE SHALL BE CHANGED."

HE'S GOT A WONDER WORKING POWER, THAT ONE!

AGAIN, IF THE DEAD GET UP, IT'S EITHER THE LAST JUDGMENT (XX FOR THOSE PLAYING ALONG AT HOME WITH THEIR TAROT DECK) OR THE VIDEO FOR "THRILLER." THE RAPTURE IS ABOUT THE LIVING SKIPPING DEATH TO GET INTO HEAVEN. BESIDES, WE ALL KNOW WHAT HAPPENS WHEN PAUL GETS A TWINKLE IN HIS EYE.
(SEE ABOVE)

OTHERS SAY IT'S INSPIRED BY THE VISIONS OF A 15-YEAR-OLD SCOTTISH GIRL NAMED MARGARET MAC DONALD. VISIONS, YOU SCOFF, DON'T KNOCK IT. MEL GIBSON MADE A FORTUNE FROM THE VISIONS OF NUNS SISTER ANNE EMMERICH AND MARY OF AGREDA, USING THEM AS THE STORY BOARD FOR HIS THE PASSION OF THE CHRIST. AND JOHN NELSON DARBY, THE MEL GIBSON OF HIS 19th CENTURY DAY, WAS JUST AS SAVVY. HE DIDN'T HAVE CELLULOID TO SPREAD HIS WORD FAR AND WIDE, SO HE TOOK TO THE SERMON CIRCUIT. BUT HE TOO LAUNCHED QUITE THE PHENOM.

"HAVE YOU BEEN SAVED, SUGAR TITS?"

REGARDLESS OF WHO OR HOW, 55% OF AMERICANS BELIEVE IN THE RAPTURE. AND TIM LAHAYE AND JERRY B. JENKINS HAVE WRITTEN A SERIES OF LEFT BEHIND BOOKS— THAT START WITH THE RAPTURE AND END WITH JESUS RIDING ACROSS THE PLAIN OF ARMAGEDDON WHILE HIS ENEMIES BURST INTO FLAMES —AND THEY'VE SOLD OVER 62 MILLION COPIES.

LIKE EVERYTHING ELSE IN AMERICA, THE RAPTURE IS BIG BUSINESS.

CHAPTER 2.6

MESHUGGE TIMES
AND
THE LEAVING IS EASY :

WORDS OF COMFORT
TO OUR
JEWISH READERS

THE MAGIC GOY IN A BLANKET
DECODER SAYS:

FOR THIS YOU LEARNED
HEBREW?

PUT THIS BOOK DOWN
AND
CALL YOUR MOTHER!

I DON'T
KNOW
MY YARMULKE
FROM
MY YAHRZEIT

למדת עברית
בשב'ל
זה?

תנ'ח לספר
והתקשר
לאמא שלך!

THE MAGIC DECODER DREIDEL SAYS:
LAMAD'TA IVRIT BISHVIL ZEH?
T'NIACH LA-SEFER V'HITKASHER
L'IMA SHELCHA!

CHAPTER 2.7

I'M CATHOLIC — DO I GO OR STAY?

PROTESTANT (OR TEAM MARTIN LUTHER), WHO ARE THE GROUP WE'RE USUALLY TALKING ABOUT WHEN WE SAY FUNDIES OR EVANGELICALS OR EVEN REPUBLICANS, SAY NO.

DESPITE THE COUNTER REFORMATION, THE JESUITS, THE KENNEDYS, OPUS DEI, AND JOHN PAUL II, THOSE WHO COTTON TO THE RAPTURE STILL HAVEN'T COTTONED TO THE CATHOLICS. THEY'RE EITHER CHRISTIANS WHO CAN'T READ THE BIBLE RIGHT (OR AT ALL) OR SERVANTS OF SATAN (WHO ELSE WOULD WEAR RED PRADA PUMPS?).

CHAPTER 2.8

WHAT'S A GOOD PAGAN GIRL (OR BOY) TO DO?

THE GOOD PAGAN
SEAL OF APPROVAL

HELL/HADES

DELIVERIES IN REAR

SEE CHAPTER 4. IN THE MEANTIME PRAY TO [YOUR FAVE DEITY GOES HERE] THAT SHE/HE/ZE WILL BRING ABOUT A REVERSE RAPTURE.

A REVERSE RAPTURE? WHAT'S THAT? YOU ASK WHILE SCRATCHING SOME PART OF YOUR BODY, PREFERABLY YOUR HEAD.

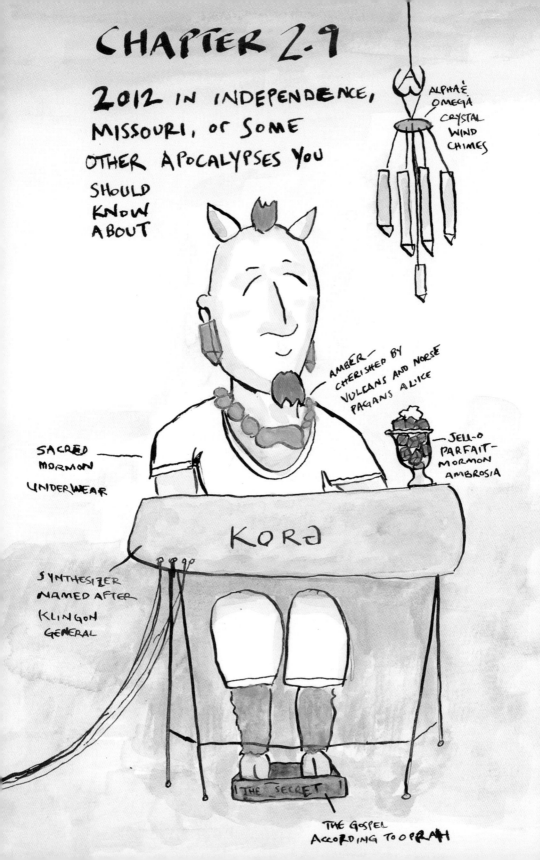

WELL, THOSE PEOPLE WHO WORSHIP AN ETERNAL
LOOP OF CHORD PROGRESSIONS PLAYED ON A SYNTHESIZER —
I BELIEVE YOU CALL THEM NEW ~~AGERS~~ AGERS —
FOR THEM, IT'S WHEN THIS 3-D WORLD WOBBLES
INTO 4-D. FOR MANY, IT'S SUPPOSED TO BE A PRETTY
BUMP,TY PHASE SHIFT. ONLY THE TRULY ALIGNED
AND RIGHTEOUS MAKE THE GRADE. THE REST GET
SHUNTED BACK TO REPEAT THE THIRD DIMENSION ON
ANOTHER PLANET. THERE'RE LOTS OF BETS THAT
THIS HAPPENS AROUND 2012 WHEN THE MAYAN
CALENDAR COMES TO AN END. (WHO KNEW IT
WAS STILL RUNNING? YOU GASP.)

OTHERS, MAINLY MORMONS, BELIEVE THAT WITH
THE SECOND COMING, CHRIST WILL SET UP HIS ZION,
HIS NEW JERUSALEM, IN INDEPENDENCE, MISSOURI —
WHICH ALSO HAPPENS TO BE THE SITE OF THE ORIGINAL
EDEN. (HOLY MÖBIUS STRIP, BATMAN!)

THIS DOES OR DOES NOT HAVE TO HAPPEN AROUND 2012,
BUT WOULDN'T THAT BE SOME COINCIDENCE.

STILL OTHERS THINK 2012 IS WHEN TIME STOPS,
THE POLES SHIFT, THE OCEANS SLOSH OUT OF
THEIR BASINS, ATLANTIS IS REVEALED, AND THINGS
GET MESSY AND NO ONE KNOWS WHAT WILL
HAPPEN NEXT.

AS FOR ME, THE REVERSE RAPTURE IS WHEN MR.
THOU SHALT NOT TAKES ALL HIS FOLLOWERS — AND THAT'S
ANYONE WHO'D KILL FOR A "SHOULD" — TO THEIR OWN
GATED DIMENSION AND LEAVES THE REST OF US TO PURSUE PAGAN
ABANDON IN PEACE.

CHAPTER 3

FUN TIME ACTIVITIES
FOR
THE
END OF TIMES

BONUS GAME: WHERE'S THE RED HEIFER?
WHAT'S ALL THIS WITH RED HEIFERS? WELL, SEEMS PER
NUMBERS 19 THEY'RE THE ULTIMATE SACRED SPOT
CLEANSER — AND SOME JEWS & CHRISTIANS THINK ONE
NEEDS TO BE SACRIFICED TO CLEAN THE TEMPLE MOUNT FOR AND
THIRD TEMPLE — PROBLEM IS, THERE'S A MOSQUE IN THE WAY THE DOME
OF THE ROCK.

1. SINCE SO MANY RAPTURE-READY FOLK LIVE IN THE U.S. of A.✱ FIND OUT WHERE MOST OF THEM LIVE. (HINT: IT'S A STATE THAT BEGINS WITH "NORTH" OR "SOUTH" AND/OR ENDS IN "O," "A," "S," OR "G."

✱ OF COURSE, ALL THE WORLD'S CHILDREN GET VACUUMED INTO HEAVEN WITH THE RAPTURE. AS FOR ADULTS, IT'S POSSIBLE THEY COULD GET AIR-LIFTED FROM COUNTRIES OUTSIDE OF THE U.S., GOD'S FAVORITE NATION-STATE AFTER ISRAEL, VATICAN CITY, SAUDIA ARABIA ...

2. PICK A HOUSE YOU REALLY LOVE AND WHOSE OCCUPANTS JUST REEK OF RIGHTEOUSNESS.

3. MOVE AS CLOSE AS POSSIBLE TO THIS HOUSE. (DON'T FORGET TO FACTOR IN WILD CARDS LIKE GLOBAL WARMING, A VERY END-TIME CLUE PHONE. SOUTH CAROLINA✱² MAY HAVE A GORGEOUS COASTLINE, BUT IT'S PROBABLY MOVING INLAND ONCE THE TRIBULATION BEGINS.)

▓ = HELL-BOUND
░ = JESUSLAND

4. WAIT

5. WHILE YOU WAIT, HOW ABOUT A GAME!

6. MOVIE NIGHT — **LEFT** BEHIND: THE MOVIE

✱² WHAT'S SO HOLY ABOUT SOUTH CAROLINA? YOU WONDER. ASK THE GOOD FOLK AT CHRISTIANEXODUS.ORG. THEY PLAN TO MAKE IT AN EVANGELICAL WILDLIFE PRESERVE.

7-12. HERE'S A DRINKING GAME TO GIVE YOU STRENGTH. PERHAPS YOU'VE PLAYED "BOB" — A DRINKING GAME WHERE YOU TAKE A SWIG OF [YOUR FAVORITE LIQUID INTOXICANT HERE] EVERY TIME SOMEONE SAYS "BOB" DURING AN EPISODE OF THE BOB NEWHART SHOW. WE TRIED TO COME UP WITH A SIMILAR GAME FOR LEFT BEHIND: THE MOVIE, STARRING BORN-AGAIN CHILD STAR KIRK CAMERON ("MIKE SEAVER" OF TV'S GROWING PAINS). OH, HOW THE SPIRIT WAS WILLING BUT THE SCRIPT WAS WEAK.

SEXY POUT OF THE ANTI-CHRIST

WE LOOKED FOR A WORD OR CATCH PHRASE THAT REPEATS. NADA. SO WE CAME UP WITH THESE WAYS TO MAKE THE VIEWING MORE BEARABLE.

- TAKE A DRINK EVERY TIME MIKE SEAVER APPEARS ON SCREEN WITH HIS WIFE.

- TAKE TWO FOR THE FIRST TIME YOU SPOT THE WORLD'S FAKEST PALM TREE.

THIS SHOULD HOLD YOU THE 30-ODD MINUTES BEFORE YOU CAN...

- TAKE A DRINK EVERY TIME A PILE OF PERFECTLY ARRANGED CLOTHES APPEARS ON SCREEN TO LET YOU KNOW SOMEONE'S BEEN RAPTURED.

- DOUBLE SHOTS WHEN THE FALLEN PILOT DISCOVERS AND CARESSES HIS RAPTURED WIFE'S NEGLIGEE AND WEDDING RING.

- TRIPLE SHOTS WHEN HE THROWS A BIBLE AT THE MIRROR.

- BONUS ROUND: FIRST PERSON TO SPOT "JAMES TRIVETTE" FROM WALKER, TEXAS RANGER DECIDES HOW MANY SHOTS THE OTHERS MUST TAKE AT THE NEXT "YOU MUST DRINK" MOMENT. (THIS SHOULD KEEP YOU DRUNK ENOUGH TO WATCH THE REST OF THE MOVIE OR FORGET IT LATER.)

13. FEELING ADVENTUROUS? PLAY THE "I HATE MYSELF" GAY VERSION. TAKE A DRINK FOR EVERY TIME KIRK CAMERON'S ASS APPEARS ONSCREEN. TAKE TWO MORE AFTERWARD AND BITCH ABOUT HOW HIS BAGGY KHAKIS ARE AS REVEALING AS A NUN'S HABIT. (HE DOESN'T DISCOVER JEANS TILL A LATER MOVIE.)

← ACTUAL ASS MAY OR MAY NOT BE WITHIN

14. DRINK FOR THE HELL OF IT AND MAKE SLURRED LEWD COMMENTS ABOUT HOW YOU'D GIVE KIRK SOMETHING TO CRY ABOUT WHEN HE DOES JUST THAT, CROUCHED ON THE FLOOR OF WHAT LOOKS TO BE A HIGH SCHOOL BATHROOM IN THE BOWELS OF THE UN.

15. DRUNKENLY PROMISE TO SWEAR OFF BORN-AGAIN TWINKS FOR THIS LIFE AND THE LIFE ETERNAL TO COME. PASS OUT WITH A VINTAGE BRUCE WEBER-PHOTOGRAPHED COPY OF THE ABERCROMBIE & FITCH CATALOG GRIPPED TIGHTLY IN ONE FIST.

POOR KIRK, HE WEEPS SO OVER YOUR SINS.

16. PICK AN ALBUM BY MICHAEL W. SMITH (AMY GRANT ON ESTROGEN) AND PLAY IT BACKWARD. (WE RECOMMEND WORSHIP OR WORSHIP AGAIN.) DOESN'T IT SOUND BETTER?

17. TO GET MORE FAMILIAR WITH RAPTUROLOGY, CREATE YOUR OWN DAVID LETTERMAN-ESQUE TOP TEN LIST. WE'LL GET YOU STARTED.

18. NUMBER TEN: YOU KNOW IT'S THE RAPTURE WHEN THE WHORES OF BABYLON AT HOOTERS SERVE UP RED HEIFER BUFFALO WINGS.

HOOTERS

19. MAKE YOUR OWN CHICK BOOKLET ABOUT THE JOYS OF [YOUR FAVORITE SIN GOES HERE] TO HAND OUT THE NEXT TIME BATTLECRY COMES TO YOUR TOWN.

20. NEVER SEEN A CHICK BOOKLET? LORD, ARE YOU HELL-BOUND! VISIT THEIR WEBSITE (WWW.CHICK.COM) OR ANY CHRISTIAN BOOKSTORE. THE ARTIST'S FAVE IS DOOM TOWN: THE STORY OF SODOM. HE SAYS THE 15th PANEL IN IS HIS APPROACHING HIS FUTURE ILLEGALLY WED HUSBAND ON THEIR FIRST DATE. NOW THAT THEY'VE BEEN MARRIED FOR 5 YEARS THEY LOOK LIKE THE 13th PANEL.

A DETAIL FROM PANEL 15

A DETAIL FROM PANEL 13

21. MOVIE NIGHT: JESUS CAMP

22. TOO GOOD A DOCUMENTARY TO POKE FUN AT. IT'S HARROW-INGLY GOOD. HOWEVER, TAKE A SWIG — TO GIVE YOU STRENGTH — WHEN YOU SEE A REAL-LIFE CHICK PAMPHLET BEING HANDED OUT BY ONE OF THE CHILDREN. IT ONLY GETS MORE INTENSE FROM THERE.

23. STILL WAITING?

24. GOOD.

25. SIGN YOUR EX UP FOR A RAPTURE LETTER (www.rapture-letters.com). IT'S DELIVERED ONCE THE RAPTURE OCCURS OR SOMEONE FORGETS TO RESET THE "DO NOT SEND" PROMPT. BETTER STILL, LET A SINFUL ATHEIST DELIVER YOUR HAND-WRITTEN LETTER TO THOSE LEFT BEHIND (www.postrapture-post.com). EXTRA HIPSTER POINTS FOR WRITING YOURSELF. ALSO OFFERS T-SHIRTS, COFFEE MUGS, AND RAPTURE SURVIVAL KIT (HOLY BIBLE).

IN CASE OF RAPTURE ADD LIQUOR

26. NEXT TIME YOU'RE IN THE MIDDLE OF NOWHERE (TOPEKA, KANSAS), PACK A SUNDAY PICKET FOR OUTSIDE FRED PHELPS'S WESTBORO BAPTIST CHURCH. FRED LOVES TO BLAME ALL THE WORLD'S ILLS — FROM 9/11 TO THE FACT THAT THE WAR IN IRAQ IS NOT GOING THE WAY JESUS'S GENERAL WOULD LIKE — ON SODOMY AND THE FAGS.

GOD HATES FAGS

IT'S ALSO HIS WEBSITE — NOT FOR THE FAINT OF HEART — SEE GODHATESFIGS.COM INSTEAD

FRED "THE SCOURGE OF ALL FUNERALS AND SWEDEN" PHELPS

27. HERE ARE SOME IDEAS FOR YOUR SIGN!

28-30.

SODOMITES MAKE BETTER LOVERS

TEMPLE PROSTITUTES FOR PIECE

GLOBAL WARMING: GOD WANTS HER PLANET BACK & SHE'LL SMOKE YOU OUT TO DO IT!

HAVE YOU HUGGED YOUR SHEKINAH TODAY?

ABOMINATION IS IN THE EYE OF THE BEHOLDER

BE GONE! YOU HAVE NO POWER HERE

WHAT WOULD LILITH DO

31. – 36: TERMINALLY ILL? TERMINALLY BLUE? DON'T WANT TO WAIT FOR AMERICA'S AMNESIA TO ALLOW GEORGE P. BUSH TO BECOME PRESIDENT IN 2016. THEN WHY NOT GO TO THE WINDOW IN ANY OF THESE PLACES AND SHOUT, "THE RAPTURE IS HAPPENING. OH MY GOD, WE'VE BEEN LEFT BEHIND!"

- WHILE HOLDING THE HAND OF SOMEONE OF THE SAME SEX YET DIFFERENT RACE ANYWHERE ON THE CAMPUS OF BOB JONES UNIVERSITY (GREENVILLE, SOUTH CAROLINA)

- WHILE ON THE 700 CLUB WITH PAT ROBERTSON OR WHILE GIVING THE COMMENCEMENT SPEECH AT HIS REGENTS UNIVERSITY (VIRGINIA BEACH, VIRGINIA)

- DITTO THE LATE JERRY FALWELL'S THOMAS ROAD BAPTIST CHURCH OR LIBERTY UNIVERSITY (LYNCHBURG, VIRGINIA)

- FROM INSIDE THE PRAYER TOWER → AT ORAL ROBERTS UNIVERSITY (TULSA, OKLAHOMA)

- INSIDE THE HEADQUARTERS OF DOMINO'S PIZZA (ANN ARBOR, MICHIGAN)

- INSIDE THE HEADQUARTERS OF PRINCE GROUP'S OFFICES, THE DEATH STAR OF ERIK PRINCE'S MERCENARY ARMY (BLACKWATER)

- INSIDE THE PURPOSE-LADEN CHURCH OF RICK WARREN (SADDLEBACK CHURCH, LAKE FOREST, CALIFORNIA)

- FROM THE HALFPIPE INSIDE STEPHEN BALDWIN'S REVIVAL MEETING TENT FOR CHRISTIAN ACTION SPORTS ENTHUSIASTS (WHEREVER THE PENTAGON-BLESSED OPERATION STRAIGHT UP AND LIVIN IT PRODUCTIONS STOP)

- ANYWHERE IN COLORADO SPRINGS, COLORADO— THE VATICAN CITY FOR EVANGELICALS — THOUGH BEST VIEWS FROM FOCUS ON THE FAMILY HEADQUARTERS OR THE AIRFORCE ACADEMY

WINDOWS FOR THE PRAYER WARRIORS

ALSO SET OF STEPHEN BALDWIN'S BIO-DOME II: THE RESURRECTION

(NEVER HEARD OF ANY OF THESE FOLKS? PICK UP A COPY OF THE SINNER'S GUIDE TO THE EVANGELICAL RIGHT BY ROBERT LANHAM. AS FUNNY AS FRIGHTENING.)

38: TRY TO WATCH THE RAPTURE ALL THE WAY THROUGH. NEITHER FELIX NOR IAN COULD. THE FIRST 30-ODD MINUTES SHOULD BE RETITLED FLATLINERS.

FABLED EYE OF NARCISSUS (OR MIRROR)

I WON'T BE IGNORED, DANA.

39: DRINK (TAKE A FEW BIG SWIGS) TO DAVID DUCHOVNY'S MULLET AND MUSCLES AND FLASH OF ASS. AFTER THAT HIGHLIGHT EITHER TRY TO KEEP WATCHING FOR THE SURREAL FINALE OR TURN OFF THE TV.

40: TIME TO ASK THE TRADITIONAL VALUES COALITION (www.traditionalvalues.org) FOR HELP CLEARING UP YOUR CONFUSION ABOUT SODOM AND GOMORRAH (THEY'RE OBSESSED WITH THE GAYS AND THAT'LL SURELY GET THEIR ATTENTION.) GIVE THEM A CALL (202-547-8570, THE DC OFFICE, OR 714-520-0300, THE ANAHEIM OFFICE) OR SEND THEM AN EMAIL (mail@traditionalvalues.org).

REVEREND "HATE THE SIN, KILL THE SINNER" LOU SHELDON, OR PAPA SMURF, OF TVC AFTER YOUR PHONE CALL

41: EXPLAIN YOU JUST READ GENESIS 19 (ALL 38 VERSES), ADD THAT ~~THAT~~ YOU UNDERSTAND THAT GOD DESTROYED SODOM AND GOMORRAH FOR BEING RUDE TO STRANGERS (NEVER A GOOD IDEA TO GANG RAPE AN ANGEL), YET GOD LET LOT ESCAPE WITH HIS DAUGHTERS. ONLY TO ALLOW HIM LATER TO GET DRUNK AND HAVE SEX WITH THEM IN A NEARBY CAVE.

42: YOUR QUESTION: DOES THIS MEAN THAT INCEST IS A TRADITIONAL FAMILY VALUE?

43: GO TO THE RAPTURE INDEX (www.raptureready.com/rap2.html). DO ONE THING TO HELP RAISE IT (CALL YOURSELF A LIBERAL ON NATIONAL TELEVISION; VOTE FOR A DEMOCRAT; VISIT AN OCCULT BOOKSTORE) OR LOWER IT (END GLOBAL WARMING; END NUCLEAR PROLIFERATION; DENOUNCE THE FALSE CHRIST NEXT DOOR).

44: GO TO RAPTURE READY (www.raptureready.com) AND COMPARE AND CONTRAST THE DOOMSDAY CLOCK (www.thebulletin.org) WITH THE ARMAGEDDON CLOCK. ONE GOES EVER-FORWARD. CAN YOU GUESS WHICH? (NEITHER REALLY AN APPROPRIATE FATHER'S DAY GIFT.)

45: STILL WAITING?

46: PATIENTLY? FAITHFULLY?

47: REALLY?

48: THEN STOP CHECKING THE TIME AT THE ARMAGEDDON CLOCK.

49 — 54: GIVE A COPY OF A BANNED BOOK TO A LIBRARY DEEP IN THE HEART OF THE BIBLE BELT (IAN RECOMMENDS TULSA, OKLAHOMA AS A GREAT PLACE TO START) OR TO THE NEXT PERSON TO HAND YOU A CHICK TRACK.

HERE ARE SOME SUGGESTIONS (ALPHABETICAL BY TITLE):

- AND TANGO MAKES THREE, JUSTIN RICHARDSON & PETER PARNELL
- A WRINKLE IN TIME, MADELEINE L'ENGLE
- BELOVED, TONI MORRISON
- BRAVE NEW WORLD, ALDOUS HUXLEY
- CANDIDE, VOLTAIRE
- CANTERBURY TALES, CHAUCER
- CATCHER IN THE RYE, JD SALINGER
- THE CHOCOLATE WAR, ROBERT CORMIER
- THE COLOR PURPLE, ALICE WALKER
- CONFESSIONS, JEAN-JACQUES ROUSSEAU
- DADDY'S ROOMMATE, MICHAEL WILLHOITE
- DECAMERON, BOCCACCIO
- FANNY HILL, JOHN CLELAND
- FOREVER, JUDY BLUME
- HARRY POTTER, ALL OF THEM, JK ROWLING
- HEATHER HAS TWO MOMMIES, LESLÉA NEWMAN
- HUCKLEBERRY FINN, MARK TWAIN
- I KNOW WHY THE CAGED BIRD SINGS, MAYA ANGELOU
- IT'S PERFECTLY NORMAL, ROBIE HARRIS
- KING & KING, LINDA DE HAAN & STERN NIJLAND
- LEAVES OF GRASS, WALT WHITMAN
- LYSISTRATA, ARISTOPHANES
- OF MICE AND MEN, JOHN STEINBECK
- ORIGIN OF SPECIES, CHARLES DARWIN
- OUTSIDERS, SE HINTON
- SCARY STORIES, ALVIN SCHWARTZ
- TO KILL A MOCKINGBIRD, HARPER LEE
- ULYSSES, JAMES JOYCE
- WHOLE LESBIAN SEX BOOK, FELICE NEWMAN
- THE WITCHES, ROALD DAHL

HARRY ENJOYS SATAN HAS TWO MOMMIES BY LUCIFER NEWMAN

55: MOVIE NIGHT: <u>VEGGIE TALES</u> (ANY DVD WILL DO. PERHAPS <u>LORD OF THE BEANS</u>™ OR <u>DAVE AND THE GIANT PICKLE</u> OR <u>AN EASTER CAROL</u> OR <u>HEROES OF THE BIBLE</u>, VOLUMES 1 OR 2.)

BOB

MEATWAD

(SEPARATED AT BIRTH?)

56: NO BOOZE THIS TIME. WE'RE GOING FOR THE HARD-CORE STUFF. UNSPIKED KOOL-AID® AND NILLA® WAFERS (A SUGAR HIGH COMMUNION). AS YOU GET GIDDIER—AND YOU WILL BEFORE YOU CRASH LIKE THE DAMNED SOUL YOU ARE— NOTICE HOW <u>AQUA TEEN HUNGER FORCE</u> IS A SECULAR RIP- OFF OF <u>VEGGIE TALES</u>. DOESN'T BOB THE TOMATO REMIND YOU OF MEATWAD?

"GLOBAL WARMING, MY LILY-WHITE HINDER. IT'S JUST THE GOOD LORD MAKING IT A LITTLE WARMER FOR US OLD FOLKS. BLESS HIM. NOW WE DON'T ALL HAVE TO MOVE TO FLORIDA."

SENATOR JAMES "GLOBAL WARMING IS A BIGGER HOAX THAN THE 2000 ELECTION" INHOFE

57–60: MAKE A DONATION TO [YOUR FAVE COOL ENVIRO GROUP HERE] IN THE NAME OF SENATOR JAMES INHOFE. (DON'T KNOW WHO HE IS? YOU SHOULD. HE KNOWS WHO YOU ARE. HE WAS THE MAYOR OF OUR ARTIST'S HOMETOWN WHEN HE WAS GROWING UP. AND OUR ARTIST CAN ATTEST THAT FOR TULSA, OKLAHOMA, INHOFE IS AS FLAMING A LIBERAL AS THEY'LL LET LIVE THERE. SENATOR COBURN OF OKLAHOMA, THE ONE WHO CAMPAIGNED FOR THE DEATH PENALTY FOR DOCTORS WHO PERFORM ABORTIONS, IS A CONSERVATIVE... DEMOCRAT... BY OKLAHOMA STANDARDS.)

61-66: DELIGHT YOUR FUNDAMENTALIST NEIGHBORS WITH A SECULAR HUMANIST CRÊCHE. (BONUS POINTS IF YOU PUT IT UP ON DARWIN'S BIRTHDAY [FEBRUARY 12] OR THE DAY THE UN CAME INTO BEING [OCTOBER 24] AND LET IT STAY UP THROUGH SATAN'S COSTUME PARTY, HALLOWEEN.)

STUMPED? HERE ARE SOME HELPFUL SUGGESTIONS FOR MAKING YOUR SECULAR HUMANIST CRÊCHE THE TALK OF THE TOWN.

THE EASIEST WAY TO BEGIN IS TO USE A CUTOUT PHOTO AND PASTE IT OVER THE CORRESPONDING PLASTIC OR WOODEN FIGURE IN YOUR TRADITIONAL NATIVITY SCENE. TRY THESE OUT FOR A NEW AND IMPROVED CAST OF CHARACTERS:

TINY INFANT BABY JESUS — REPLACE THE BABY WITH A COPY OF THE BILL OF RIGHTS OR THE UTNE READER

MARY — CAMILLE PAGLIA OR HILARY RODHAM CLINTON

JOSEPH — RICHARD DAWKINS OR BILL CLINTON

SHEPHERDS — KARL MARX, MICHEL FOUCAULT, KEITH OLBERMANN OR PAPA SMURF

WISE MEN (PICK ANY THREE) — CHARLES DARWIN, CLARENCE DARROW (THOUGH NO ONE ON EITHER SIDE KNOWS WHO HE IS TODAY), THOMAS PAINE (DITTO), KOFI ANNAN, HUGO CHÁVEZ, GEORGE SOROS, SEYMOUR HERSH, JON STEWART, BILL MOYERS, JIMMY CARTER, BARACK OBAMA, AL GORE

ANGEL — MOLLY IVINS, ARIANNA HUFFINGTON, OPRAH

ANIMALS — LEAVE AS IS, THOUGH YOU CAN PUT BILL O'REILLY'S FACE OVER THE DONKEY.

MOTHER OF GOD '68

67: IMBIBE A MIND-ALTERING SUBSTANCE (WINE, COFFEE, RED BULL, THE RUNOFF FROM A BOWL OF COCOA KRISPIES) AND WATCH A BIT OF JAN CROUCH ON TBN. DOES HER HAIR TALK TO YOU, TOO?

68: BECOME AN ORDAINED MINISTER IN THE UNIVERSAL LIFE CHURCH (www.themonastery.org). THE ONLINE ORDINATION IS FREE. ONCE YOU'RE ORDAINED, DEMAND THAT ALL YOUR CONSERVATIVE FRIENDS AND RELATIVES CALL YOU ▬▬▬ REVEREND [YOUR FIRST AND/OR LAST NAME HERE] FROM NOW ON. BETTER STILL, MAKE IT OFFICIAL WITH SOMETHING TO FORCE MOM AND DAD TO HANG ON THE WALL. FOR UNDER $20 YOU CAN GET A LOVELY BESTOWAL OF TITLE CERTIFICATE PROCLAIMING YOU ANYTHING FROM AN ABBESS TO A GODDESS, FROM A MAGUS TO A PROPHET, FROM A RABBI TO A WIZARD.

PATRIARCH LILITH

69: GET HIPSTER CRED OUT THE ASS AND MAYBE A LOVE LETTER FROM DAN SAVAGE BY MARRYING A MAN (PREFERABLY GAY) TO A DOG NAMED RICK SANTORUM.

70: WAIT WITH GLACIAL CALM. (BE SURE TO CHANNEL OLD-SCHOOL, PRE-GLOBAL-WARMING GLACIERS. NEW SCHOOL JUST CRACK TOO EASILY UNDER PRESSURE.)

71: WHEN THE SKY OVERHEAD BREAKS INTO A HEAVENLY CHORUS, TAKE A DEEP BREATH. BUT DON'T CLOSE YOUR EYES! IT'S ALL GONNA HAPPEN IN THE BLINK OF AN EYE. (OF COURSE, NO ONE SPECIFIED IF THAT'S A HUMAN EYE BLINK OR GOD'S. AND MANY ARE CONVINCED HIS LID HAS BEEN DOWN FOR SEVERAL MILLENNIA AND ARE NOT SURE WHEN IT WILL LIFT. AGAIN, WAIT AND HAVE FAITH.)

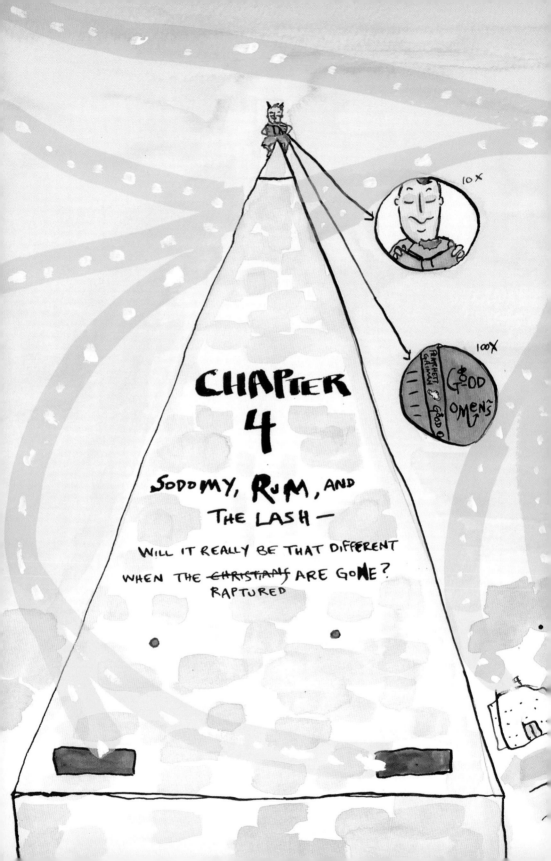

10X

100X

RAMPSETT GAIMAN GOOD O

GOOD OMENS

CHAPTER 4

SODOMY, RUM, AND THE LASH —

WILL IT REALLY BE THAT DIFFERENT WHEN THE ~~CHRISTIANS~~ ARE ~~GONE~~?
RAPTURED

HAPPY ReVerse Rapture!

IAN PHILIPS IS A RATHER RUN-OF-THE-MILL SODOMITE AND BORN-AGAIN WITCH FROM TULSA, OKLAHOMA, THAT HULKING RHINESTONE GLUED TO THE BUCKLE OF THE BIBLE BELT, WHERE HE WENT UNDER THE DRAG NAME OF WAYNE ROBERT GOBLE, III. HE NOW GROWS BOOKS WITH HIS ILLEGALLY WED HUSBAND, GREG WHARTON, IN THE "FRUIT HILLS" OF OAKLAND.

FELIX RUMPUS IS THE HEADMASTER OF HARD HOOVES SCHOOL OF MAGIC SATIRE. HE HOPES THIS IS THE FIRST OF KAJILLIONS OF BOOKS. HIS MOTTO IS: "IF IT LOOKS GOOD ON BEVERLY LAHAYE, IT'LL LOOK EVEN BETTER ON TIM." HE WELCOMES NEW FRIENDS AT:

http://www.myspace.com/reverserapture